Who Feels Mad, Dear Dragon?

by Margaret Hillert
Illustrated by Jack Pullan

NORWOOD HOUSE PRESS

DEAR CAREGIVER, The *Beginning-to-Read* series is comprised of carefully written books that extend the collection of classic readers you may remember from your own childhood. Each book features text comprised of common sight words to provide your child ample practice reading the words that appear most frequently in written text. The many additional details in the pictures enhance the story and offer the opportunity for you to help your child expand oral language and develop comprehension.

Begin by reading the story to your child, followed by letting him or her read familiar words and soon your child will be able to read the story independently. At each step of the way, be sure to praise your reader's efforts to build his or her confidence as an independent reader. Discuss the pictures and encourage your child to make connections between the story and his or her own life. At the end of the story, you will find reading activities and a word list that will help your child practice and strengthen beginning reading skills.

Above all, the most important part of the reading experience is to have fun and enjoy it!

Shannon Cannon

Shannon Cannon, Ph.D., Literacy Consultant

Norwood House Press • P.O. Box 316598 • Chicago, Illinois 60631
For more information about Norwood House Press please visit our website at
www.norwoodhousepress.com or call 866-565-2900.
Text copyright ©2018 by Margaret Hillert. Illustrations and cover design copyright ©2018 by
Norwood House Press, Inc. All rights reserved. No part of this book may be reproduced or utilized
in any form or by any means without written permission from the publisher.

LIBRARY OF CONGRESS CATALOGING-IN-PUBLICATION DATA
Names: Hillert, Margaret, author. | Pullan, Jack, illustrator.
Title: Who feels mad, Dear Dragon? / by Margaret Hillert ; illustrated by
    Jack Pullan.
Description: Chicago, IL : Norwood House Press, [2017] | Series: A
    beginning-to-read book | Summary: "A boy and his pet dragon feel mad when
    asked to do daily tasks. Together they learn to manage their anger and
    find that completing their tasks is a good thing. This title includes
    reading activities and a word list"-- Provided by publisher.
Identifiers: LCCN 2016052216 (print) | LCCN 2017018257 (ebook) | ISBN
    9781684040056 (eBook) | ISBN 9781599538228 (library edition : alk. paper)
Subjects: | CYAC: Anger--Fiction. | Family life--Fiction. | Dragons--Fiction.
Classification: LCC PZ7.H558 (ebook) | LCC PZ7.H558 Wgu 2017 (print) | DDC
    [E]--dc23
LC record available at https://lccn.loc.gov/2016052216

Hardcover ISBN: 978-1-59953-822-8   Paperback ISBN: 978-1-68404-000-1

302N—072017
Manufactured in the United States of America in North Mankato, Minnesota.

Time to come in and eat.

No! No!
Mother, do I have to?
I do not want to come in.

Do not get mad.
You will like this.

5

Yes this is good.
Thank you, Mother.

It is almost bedtime.
Time to get ready for bed.

No! No!
Mother, I do not want to.
I want to play with my toys.

Do not get mad.
You can play with your toys
in the bath tub.

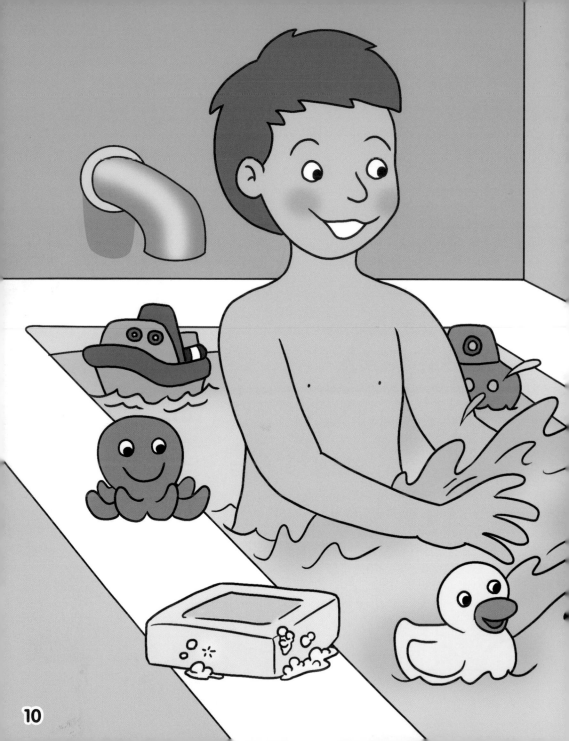

This is fun.
I like to take a bath.

Bath time is over.
Time to brush your teeth.

No! No!
I do not want to brush my teeth.

Do not get mad.
I will brush my teeth, too.
It is good to do.

I see.
My teeth feel clean.
This is good.

Now you are ready for bed.
Come here. Come here.

No! No!
I want Father to read me a book.
Father! Father!

Yes. Yes.
I will read you a book.
How about the book with cars?

No! No!
I do not want that one!

Do not get mad.
You will like it.

21

That book was good.
I like cars.

Now it is time to sleep.
Good night!

No, no!
I do not want to sleep!

Do not get mad.
Go to sleep.
It is good to sleep.

Good morning, Mother!
Good morning, Father!
Today will be a good day.
I will not get mad.

Here you are with me.
And here I am with you.
Oh what a good day it will be,
Dear Dragon.

The following activities support the findings of the National Reading Panel that determined the most effective components for reading instruction are: Phonemic Awareness, Phonics, Vocabulary, Fluency, and Text Comprehension.

Phonemic Awareness: The /m/ sound

Sound Substitution: Say the /**m**/ sound for your child. Read each word below to your child and ask your child to say the word without the /**m**/ sound:

mad – /m/ = ad   Mother – /m/ = other   mice – /m/ = ice

man – /m/ = an   many – /m/ = any   mask – /m/ = ask

meat – /m/ = eat   mat – /m/ = at

Phonics: Word Ladder

Word ladders are a fun way to build words by changing just one letter at a time. Write the word 'ad' on a piece of paper and give your child the following step-by-step instructions (the letters between the / / marks indicate that you are to give the sound as a clue rather than providing the actual letter):

- add the /m/ sound to the beginning of the word. What do you have? (mad)
- change the /m/ to a /s/. What do you have? (sad)
- change the /d/ to a /t/. What do you have? (sat)
- change the /s/ to a /c/. What do you have? (cat)

Vocabulary: Concept Words

1. Fold a piece of paper vertically in half.

2. Draw a line down the fold to divide the paper in two parts.

3. Write the words good and bad in separate columns at the top of the page.

4. Write the following statements on separate pieces of paper:

   brushing your teeth   leaving a mess   taking a bath

   not making your bed   listening to your parents playing nicely

   staying up past bedtime   asking nicely for something

5. Read each statement aloud and ask your child whether the action belongs in the good or bad column.

6. Encourage your child to add additional good and bad behaviors seen at home and school.

Fluency: Choral Reading

1. Reread the story with your child at least two more times while your child tracks the print by running a finger under the words as they are read. Ask your child to read the words he or she knows with you.

2. Reread the story aloud together. Be careful to read at a rate that your child can keep up with.

3. Repeat choral reading and allow your child to be the lead reader and ask him or her to change from a whisper to a loud voice while you follow along and change your voice.

Text Comprehension: Discussion Time

1. Ask your child to retell the sequence of events in the story.

2. To check comprehension, ask your child the following questions:

   • Why was the boy mad on page 8?

   • Why is it good to brush your teeth?

   • When you get mad, what are things you can do to stop feeling mad?

WORD LIST

Who Feels Mad, Dear Dragon? uses the 73 words listed below.
The **5** words bolded below serve as an introduction to new vocabulary, while the other 68 are pre-primer. You may wish to write the words on index cards and use them to help your child build automatic word recognition. Regular practice with these words will enhance your child's fluency in reading connected text.

a	day	have	**night**	take	want
about	dear	here	no	**teeth**	was
almost	do	how	not	thank	what
am	dragon		now	that	will
and		I		the	with
are	eat	in	oh	this	
		is	one	time	yes
bath	father	it	over	to	you
be	feel			today	your
bed	for	like	play	too	
bedtime	fun			toys	
book		mad	read	tub	
brush	get	me	ready		
	go	**morning**			
can	good	mother	see		
cars		my	sleep		
clean					
come					

ABOUT THE AUTHOR   Margaret Hillert has helped millions of children all over the world learn to read independently. She was a first grade teacher for 34 years and during that time started writing books that her students could both gain confidence in reading and enjoy. She wrote well over 100 books for children just learning to read. As a child, she enjoyed writing poetry and continued her poetic writings as an adult for both children and adults.

Photograph by Glenna Washburn

ABOUT THE ILLUSTRATOR   A talented and creative illustrator, Jack Pullan, is a graduate of William Jewell College. He has also studied informally at Oxford University and the Kansas City Art Institute. He was mentored by the renowned watercolor artists, Jim Hamil and Bill Amend. Jack's work has graced the pages of many enjoyable children's books, various educational materials, cartoon strips, as well as many greeting cards. Jack currently resides in Kansas.